Words by
Jeanne Willis

Illustrations by
Adam Stower

BARRON'S

The Wheels on the Bus

All aboard!
All aboard!

The WHEELS on the bus go **round** and **round**,
Round and **round**, **round** and **round**.
The WHEELS on the bus go **round** and **round**
at the ZOO.

The BEAR on the bus goes **brum brum brum,**
Brum brum brum, brum brum brum.
The BEAR on the bus goes **brum brum brum**
at the ZOO.

The PENGUIN on the bus goes *flip* flap **FLOP**,
Flip flap **FLOP**, *flip* flap **FLOP**.
The PENGUIN on the bus goes *flip* flap **FLOP**
at the ZOO.

The WARTHOG on the bus goes
snort snort SNEEZE,
Snort snort SNEEZE,
snort snort SNEEZE.
The WARTHOG on the bus goes
snort snort SNEEZE
at the ZOO.

The HIPPOS on the bus go *squish* squash SQUEEZE,

Squish squash SQUEEZE, *squish* squash SQUEEZE.

The HIPPOS on the bus go *squish* squash SQUEEZE, at the ZOO.

The TIRES on the bus go *hiss* BANG POP!

Hiss BANG POP! Hiss BANG POP!

The TIRES on the bus go *hiss*

BANG

POP!

at

the

zoo.

The CREATURES on the bus tip **upside** *down,*
Upside *down,* **upside** *down.*
The CREATURES on the bus tip **upside** *down*
at the
ZOO.

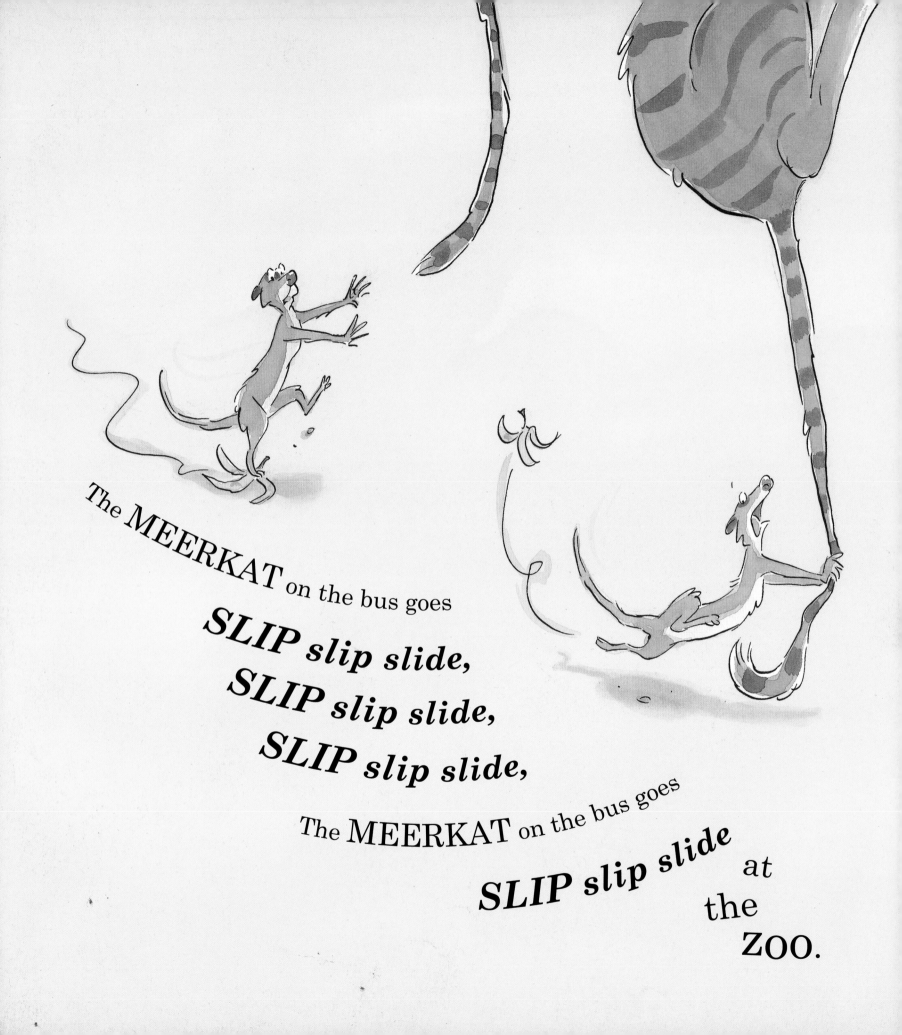

The MEERKAT on the bus goes
SLIP *slip slide,*
SLIP *slip slide,*
SLIP *slip slide,*

The MEERKAT on the bus goes
SLIP *slip slide* at
the
ZOO.

The SKUNK on the bus goes *stink stink stink,*

Stink stink stink,

stink stink stink.

The SKUNK on the bus goes

Stink stink stink

at

the

ZOO.

The OWL on the bus goes **blink wink blink,**
Blink wink blink, blink wink blink.
The OWL on the bus goes **blink wink blink**
at the ZOO.

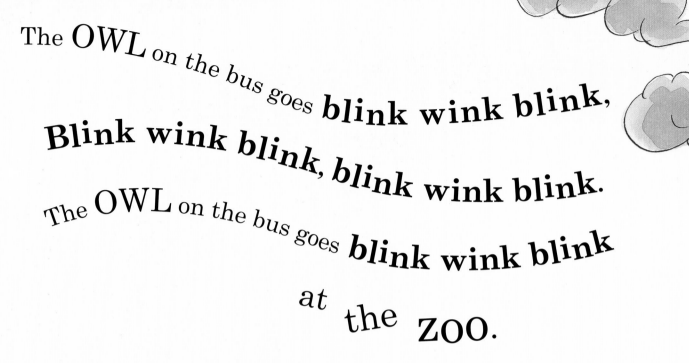

"Everybody off.
No pushing please!"

The ELEPHANT on the bus goes *puff puff puff*,
Puff puff puff, puff puff puff.
The ELEPHANT on the bus goes *puff puff puff*
at the ZOO.

The CREATURES on the bus go **clap clap clap**,
Clap clap clap, clap clap clap.
The CREATURES on the bus go
clap clap clap
at the ZOO.

All aboard!
All aboard!
And off we GO!

The WHEELS on the bus go **round** and **round**,
Round and **round**, **round** and **round**.
The WHEELS on the bus go **round** and **round**
at the ZOO.

For Rafe Peacock—J.W.

For Tamlyn, Caroline and Alison
who keep the wheels going round—A.S.

First edition for the United States, its dependencies, and the Philippines published in 2012 by Barron's Educational Series, Inc.

First published in the United Kingdom by Puffin Books, 2012
Puffin Books
Published by the Penguin Group: London, New York, Australia, Canada, India, Ireland, New Zealand and South Africa
Penguin Books Ltd, Registered Office: 80 Strand, London WC2R 0RL, England
Text copyright © Jeanne Willis 2012
Illustrations copyright © Adam Stower 2012

All inquiries should be addressed to:
Barron's Educational Series, Inc.
250 Wireless Boulevard
Hauppauge, New York 11788
www.barronseduc.com

ISBN: 978-0-7641-6491-0
Library of Congress Control No.: 2011935798

Date of Manufacture: January 2012
Manufactured by: HESHAN ASTROS PRINTING LTD, Industrial Development Area,
Xijiang River, Gulao Town, Heshan, Guangdong, China

Printed in China
9 8 7 6 5 4 3 2 1